Voyagers of the
Silver Sand

A Magical World Awaits You
Read

THE
SECRETS
OF
DROON

Voyagers of the Silver Sand

by Tony Abbott

Illustrated by David Merrell

Cover illustration by Tim Jessell

A
LITTLE APPLE
PAPERBACK

SCHOLASTIC INC.
New York Toronto London Auckland Sydney
Mexico City New Delhi Hong Kong Buenos Aires

For more information about the continuing saga of Droon,
please visit Tony Abbott's website at
www.tonyabbottbooks.com

ISBN 0-439-67177-9

Text copyright © 2005 by Robert T. Abbott.
Illustrations copyright © 2005 by Scholastic Inc.

To Linda and Rob
and Brian and Victoria
with greatest affection

Contents

One

The Hidden Stairs

BLAM! The earth exploded in front of Eric Hinkle and sent him tumbling down a riverbank into his friends. "Oof! Sorry!"

"Hey, my foot!" said Neal Kroger, sliding down behind him.

"Your foot! How about my knee?" said Julie Rubin, crawling out from beneath them both.

"How about we stop complaining and

run?" said Princess Keeah. "The beasts are coming!"

"And getting closer all the time," chirped Max, the spider troll. "Look!"

His head aching from the explosion, Eric peeked over the top of the riverbank and saw an army of furry, gray, lion-shaped beasts charging across the plains toward them. Their eyes blazed bright red.

They were the beasts of Emperor Ko.

"Man," Eric grumbled. "It's almost as if they don't like us or something."

"No kidding!" said Keeah. "But if we keep running, maybe we can hold out until my parents and Khan find us. Let's move!"

Right. Keeah's parents, King Zello and Queen Relna, and Khan, leader of the purple, pillow-shaped Lumpies, had been with the kids not too long ago. They'd all been chasing Ko's evil floating palace when they were attacked. The king and queen were driven away, and now the kids were trapped at the river.

"I hope this works," said Julie.

"Cross your fingers, everyone!" said Neal.

As the five friends scuttled quickly down the river, Eric's mind raced over everything that had happened in the last hour.

He was in Droon, of course. Where else would he, his friends, a wizard princess, and a spider troll be running from an army of nasty, red-eyed beasts?

Splashhh! The water exploded behind them.

"They know where we are!" squeaked Max, his orange hair standing straight up. "Hurry!"

Droon was the magical world Eric, Julie, and Neal had discovered one day in his basement. Ever since they had descended a mysterious rainbow-colored staircase, they'd had one fabulous adventure after another.

It was on their very first visit to Droon that they met Keeah, a young wizard just learning her powers. Along with her friend Max and the great old wizard Galen, Keeah had worked hard to keep Droon free.

"Change of plan!" she said, scrambling behind an outcropping of rock. "We'll have to make a stand here." She turned and gave Eric a little smile. "Time to uncross those fingers, pal!"

Eric looked at his fingers.

Yes, that was part of the adventure, too. Since coming to Droon, Eric had developed his own wizard powers. He could cast spells, shoot powerful sparks from his fingertips, read mysterious old languages, and even have visions of the future.

So far, having powers had been pretty cool.

Julie had gained some powers, too. She had developed the ability to fly and to alter her shape. Meanwhile, Neal was still waiting and hoping for powers of his own. But together all three friends had helped Keeah fight the bad guys time and time again.

For most of that time, the worst bad guy was a sorcerer named Lord Sparr. Since the beginning, he had struggled against Keeah and her friends to take control of Droon. But when Sparr used his Three Powers to wake up his former master, Emperor Ko, he accidentally turned himself back into a boy.

Sparr was now helping them battle Ko!

That had been going pretty well. Until the impossible happened.

Crouching behind the rock, Eric looked

at his watch. The impossible had happened exactly one hour and seven minutes ago.

His blood ran cold when he thought about it.

At the end of their last adventure, young Sparr had fled Ko and escaped on a magical river that flowed all the way up to Eric's town in the Upper World.

Unfortunately, Ko's second-in-command, an evil dragon named Gethwing, had chased right after Sparr. When the kids raced to the rainbow stairs to follow them, Ko had uttered a terrible curse.

"Selat-panoth-ra-ka-Saba!"

A few moments later, the staircase wobbled.

It sizzled.

It fizzled.

And then it vanished.

Vanished!

Eric couldn't believe it. No one could

believe it. But there was nothing they could do. The rainbow stairs were the only path between the Upper World and Droon. Even though Sparr and Gethwing were in the Upper World, the kids were trapped in Droon. They couldn't return home until the stairs returned. *If* they returned.

My parents! he thought. *My house! My town!*

Luckily, no time passed at home while the kids were in Droon. So everything would stay the way they left it. At least Eric hoped so.

"Incoming fireball," cried Neal. "Duck!"

BLAMMM! A bolt of light exploded in front of them, and Eric fell back to the ground.

"Oww, my head! Keeah! Julie? Guys —"

They didn't answer.

Blinking his eyes and rubbing his nose, he sat up and looked around.

"What —" he whispered.

He wasn't by the riverbank anymore. His friends were gone. So was the daylight. He was sitting on dark, wet ground in the middle of a starless, moonless night.

Eric staggered to his feet. As his eyes adjusted to the darkness, he began to make out the shapes of giant boulders and broken rocks strewn all around.

"This isn't good," he said. "Where am I?"

A mass of twisted trees loomed on his right, while on his left a flaming stump bloomed with dense smoke. Far away, he could see the dim outlines of a seacoast with wild black waves crashing.

Closing his eyes, Eric rubbed his forehead.

Then he remembered the explosion.

And it all made sense.

"Of course! I'm having a vision. I hit

my head and now I'm seeing . . . the Dark Lands!"

The Dark Lands.

Smelly, smoky, always foggy, always scary, the Dark Lands had been the center of evil in Droon for centuries.

Waving the smoke away, he turned, stumbled over a low stump, and nearly fell again. "The Dark Lands! What a mess! How can anybody live like this?"

"You tell me!" hissed a sudden voice.

Eric whirled around.

Out of the haze stepped an eight-foot-tall, black-scaled dragon with four sharp wings jutting up from its shoulders. Raising its massive head, the dragon grinned at him.

Eric stepped back. "Gethwing?"

"The one and only!" said the moon dragon.

Eric narrowed his eyes. "Wait. My visions tell the future. You're supposed to be in my world. Why are you back here in the Dark Lands —"

Drool from the dragon's fangs hissed as it struck the ground. "The Dark Lands? Oh, no, no, no. Take another look, Wizard Boy. . . ."

"What?" Eric turned completely around, then back again. He saw a forest, a field, a dip in the land, and a coast in the distance.

Eric's head hurt again suddenly.

Closing his eyes, he blinked them open and squinted more carefully this time.

He took several steps forward through the rocks. Then he turned, looked left, then right, stumbled another few steps, and stopped.

His heart thudded in his chest.

"Impossible," he said.

But there was no mistaking it. He was

standing just a few feet away from . . . from where his house was supposed to be!

From where it *should* have been.

From where it *would* have been. Unless . . .

The sound of his blood thundered in his ears. "But my parents? My town? What did you do?"

Gethwing grinned. "I huffed and I puffed and, well, you know the rest."

Eric's fingertips sprinkled hot silver sparks. "This can't be true. No way. If this is the future, I can change it. And I'm going to change it right now. I'm going to get rid of you!"

"But this is a vision. You can't hurt me," said the dragon. "Besides, I'm up here in your world, and you're really down there in Droon. You can't be in two places at once —"

"No, no, no!"

Just as Eric raised his sparking hands . . .

. . . *BLAMMM!* The air exploded again, and he was flat on his back once more.

When he opened his eyes, it was day again, and his friends were dragging him behind the large rock.

"Dude, I did say, 'Duck,'" said Neal. "You nearly got fried."

He blinked. "Uh . . . wow!"

"Is your head okay?" asked Keeah.

"You took a nasty tumble!" chirped Max.

Eric gazed at his friends, then squinted down the river. The lions were still charging, sending blazing beams from their eyes.

Blam! Blammm!

"Whoa, guys," he said. "I had a vision. I was in the Upper World, only there was nothing left. Gethwing had destroyed it all!"

Blam! Chunks of rock fell on the kids.

"If it was only a vision," said Julie, "it hasn't happened yet. But these beasts are here right now, and you have to blast back —"

Suddenly, they heard the sound of hooves splashing up the river behind them. A trio of shaggy white pilkas was coming up fast.

"Reinforcements!" cried Neal. "Yay!"

Queen Relna, King Zello, and Khan were galloping at the head of an enormous troop of blue-clad, bow-toting soldiers.

"Archers — fire!" boomed Zello.

From their saddles, the soldiers shot a sizzling barrage of arrows at the gray lions.

Thwink-thwink-thwink! The arrows formed a wall in front of the beasts, halting their attack.

"Mother, Father," said Keeah, running to them. "You came just in time —"

"We hope we're in time," said Relna. She hopped down from her pilka and opened her saddlebag. "While we were chasing

Ko, a messenger came to us from the Guardians. They have been searching for you for the last hour."

"Bodo and Vasa?" asked Julie.

The two Guardians lived in the flying city of Ro, which soared over Droon invisibly, except for one day a year, when it landed in the Kalahar Valley.

Khan nodded. "They asked you to come at once. The city is landing today. The Guardians know how to restore the staircase —"

"They do?" gasped Eric. "Then what are we waiting for? Let's go!"

The archers rode up the embankment and fired yet another round of arrows. Howling, the beasts retreated even farther.

"We'll send these lions packing, then meet you in Ro," said Zello. "Before we lost sight of the emperor's floating palace, he was heading for Ro, too. Relna?"

The queen quickly took four bundles from her backpack. In a twinkling, each bundle unwrapped itself into a colorful little carpet.

Keeah beamed. "Pasha's Mini-Speeders. They're *very* fast. Faster than fast, in fact!"

"I call the one with stars," said Neal, plopping onto a bright little rug.

"Max, you can come with me," said Julie.

"Gladly," he said. "Keeah, lead the way!"

Eric jumped onto a small maroon rug. "If there's any way to bring back the staircase, we have to do it," he said. "We need to get home before my vision becomes real."

"We will," Keeah vowed.

"Beware of wingsnakes," said Khan. "Ko's fiery snakes are always first to attack!"

"We'll watch out," said Julie. "Carpets, go!"

Whoosh! The magic carpets lifted up from the riverbank, wobbled for a second, then shot away across the sky.

Two

City out of the Clouds

True to their name, Pasha's carpets flew faster than fast. Within minutes, the five friends had spotted a range of purple hills.

"Kalahar Valley just ahead," chirped Max. "Look how its magical diamonds glitter."

The city of Ro needed the diamonds to keep it flying and to protect its Tower of Memory, where the history of Droon was written.

"And look behind us," said Julie, as a dark swarm took shape in the sky behind them.

"Wingsnakes!" said Keeah.

The flying snakes of Emperor Ko had spiky tails and wings of flame, and they announced themselves with high-pitched shrieks. *Eeeeee!*

"Bandits at six o'clock!" cried Neal, jerking around as the swarm swept closer. "And at two-thirty. Also about twenty to four —"

"They're everywhere!" shouted Max.

"Outrun them," said Keeah. "After me!"

Zip! Whoosh! Yanking her carpet this way and that, the princess led the small group up and around the hills surrounding the vast Kalahar Valley.

The wingsnakes tried to keep up, but the kids weaved Pasha's carpets in and out of the hills too quickly. Shrieking one last time, the beasts drifted back into the hills.

"Ha-ha," said Neal. "That'll show them."

"And not a minute too soon," said Eric. "The flying city is coming. There. Look!"

At first, all they saw was a blur in the air. Then it seemed as if someone was moving a piece of cloudy glass across the sky. Finally, the air thickened, a high wall formed, and dozens of onion-shaped domes appeared.

Overshadowing everything was the giant Tower of Memory, a coiling mass of stone rising from the middle of a great palace.

"Let's get down there," said Julie, "before those overgrown worms come back."

Fwoosh! One after the other, the carpets descended into the city. Sweeping over domes and under archways, the friends finally glided down to the ground in front of the palace.

At once, the main courtyard filled with squat, bright-suited, red-haired Rovians.

"Princess Keeah and friends!" chirped one creature in a yellow helmet. "Vasa and Bodo await you in the engine room. Everyone else, battle stations. Ko is coming! Pip-pop-pip!"

As the Rovians pipped and popped and rushed into action, Keeah leaped from her carpet and charged up the steps. "Vasa and Bodo need our help. Let's move it."

Eric raced right behind her. *They need our help*? he thought. *I think we need their help, too!*

Drawn by terrible clanking and whirring sounds, the five friends hurried through corridors and up and down stairs until they came to a large door at the end of a long hallway. Noise thundered from inside.

"Lots of banging and pounding," said Neal.

"Sounds like the engine room," said Julie.

Opening the door, they entered a chamber of spinning gears and puffing smokestacks. Two tall lizards wearing green robes were busily working an array of giant controls.

Keeah ran over to them. "Bodo, Vasa, we came as soon as we could!"

Vasa, the shorter of the two Guardians, turned his great head. "Behold our diamond motor!" he shouted over the machine's roar. "We can't fly invisibly without diamonds!"

"And we can't do anything at all if Ko decides to move in!" said his fellow Guardian. Bodo pushed a pair of tiny glasses up on his big snout and whispered to a tiny Rovian nearby.

The creature listened intently, then tugged on a big lever. At once, the floor quaked.

"Good," said Bodo, waving to a far door.

"Our flight plan will buy us some time before Ko comes. Now, on to important matters. Children, to the Tower! Quickly!"

Without another word, the two Guardians swept through a series of narrow halls. The kids hurried after them. After many turns, they passed under a tall arch and into the Tower of Memory.

The moment they entered the circular structure, Eric felt his fingers tingle. He knew that on the Tower stones were written stories about everything that had ever happened in Droon. Seeing his and his friends' names, he remembered the stories as if they had happened yesterday. The time they battled the hawk bandits of Tarkoom. The voyage they took on Keeah's ship, the *Jaffa Wind*. And who could forget the sleeping giant of Goll?

"The whole history of Droon is here," he said. "This Tower seems so alive."

"It sort of is," said Neal, squinting to the top. "Quill is still writing stuff, isn't he?"

Vasa smiled. "And he's been busy lately!"

Quill was the magical feather pen who had written Droon's history on the stones. Even now, the pen could be heard scratching away at the very top of the Tower.

"It's so beautiful here," said Julie. "Why does Ko want to destroy it?"

Bodo smiled slightly. "Destroy it? I'm afraid it's not quite as simple as that." From a little space in the wall, he removed a small wooden chest. He flipped open the lid. The chest was empty. "We have been robbed," he said.

"My gosh," said Keeah. "What was stolen? What happened?"

Vasa took a deep breath. "Something we had always thought impossible," he said. "At the very moment Ko uttered his

curse on the staircase, a horrible beast named Saba entered the Tower and stole five small but very important treasures from this box."

"What are the treasures?" asked Eric.

Bodo shook his head. "We never knew. Hours before he disappeared in the city of Ut, Galen gave us five unique treasures sealed in this chest. He said that without these treasures, the staircase would never have existed. And that only these treasures would restore the staircase if it was ever lost. Galen put this chest in the Tower for safekeeping. Unfortunately, the treasures were not safe from Saba."

"But that's not all," added Vasa. He pointed to five stones in different places on the tower walls. The stones had been wiped clean, as if there had never been any writing on them.

"On these stones were written a story

called the Legend of the Five Treasures," said Vasa. "When Saba stole the treasures, this story vanished from our history. The Legend of the Five Treasures disappeared."

The children looked at one another. "So it's simple," said Eric finally. "We need to get those treasures back."

"That's exactly what you must do," said Vasa. He stepped onto the stairs and began to climb to the top. "But it's not so simple."

"No," said Bodo, climbing after his fellow Guardian, "for the Legend of the Five Treasures is set in the land of Eshku."

Max hastened after the Guardians. "Eshku? Excuse me. I've been over all of Droon, and I never once heard of a place called Eshku!"

Vasa chuckled. "That's because Eshku is not so much a place . . . as it is a time."

"A time!" Neal laughed. Then he

stopped. "Wait. Am I the only one getting a headache?"

"In fact, Eshku is five times," said Vasa. "It is a desert land five centuries long. It is what's known in Droon as . . . *a country of the past!*"

The children followed the two tall lizards up the steps without speaking.

"Simply put, you must travel back into the history of Droon," said Bodo. They were nearing the top of the Tower. "Only there will you find the treasures. If you find them and bring them back, the old legend will be rewritten, and the stairs will return. If not, Ko will control the stairs forever."

"But beware," added Vasa, "for so surely as you enter Eshku, Saba himself will be there to make sure you fail."

"Already I don't like this Saba guy," said Neal. "Who is he?"

"Ah, yes, I knew someone would ask,"

said Bodo, his face grim. "Saba is Ko's phantom, an exact double of the emperor in every way, except that he bears no shadow. Being a phantom, Saba can travel in space and time to wherever and whenever he is sent. With Saba doing Ko's dirty work, the emperor can be in two places at once!"

Eric shivered. Gethwing had said in his vision that Eric couldn't be in two places at once. But Ko could be. Great. So now the beast emperor was suddenly twice as dangerous.

Max frowned. "Neal, I think your headache is catching."

"There's enough to go around," said Neal.

"Of course, you won't be completely on your own," said Vasa. "None other than Galen himself appears in each and every story!"

"My master?" chirped Max. "Well, that changes things. You mean we could meet Galen at five different ages? He's been gone so long. It would be wonderful to see him again. Princess, can we go?"

The children looked at one another for a long time. Finally, they nodded together.

"I think we're going to Eshku!" said Keeah.

Bodo smiled. "Excellent! And there is someone else to help you. Since you must rewrite these stories, who better to go with you than our magical feather pen himself? He will be your guide into the past —"

Suddenly, ear-piercing shrieks shattered the air. *Eeeeee!*

"Wingsnakes!" said Max, looking up. "At the top of the Tower."

"And they're attacking Quill!" cried Eric. "To the top — now!"

Three

Deserts of the Past

Eric, Keeah, Julie, Neal, and Max shot past the Guardians and raced up the Tower. But when they got to the top, they found three wingsnakes flailing wildly and dripping ink from their faces. Quill, the silvery-white feather pen, stood firmly on the wall.

"That'll teach you to fight me!" he snapped. "Now, be gone, or I'll squirt you again!"

Eeeee! the wingsnakes wailed. Their eyes blazed and their wings flamed, but they fled quickly from the Tower and into the clouds.

"Humf!" squeaked the pen. "So there!"

Keeah blinked. "Quill! You're safe? And . . . you talk!"

The feather wiggled and bowed. "Talk. Recite poems. Sing. And apparently, I can fight, too!"

Vasa smiled and held out his hand. Quill hopped into his palm. "May I present your chronicler and your guide? Quill will write the new stories you make. Bodo and I found a charm to give Quill a voice —"

"A squeaky little voice," whispered Bodo.

"I heard that," snapped the feather pen. "So I must have ears, too —"

Suddenly, the city began to tilt.

"We're speeding up," said Neal.

"Which means that Ko's floating palace is in sight," said Bodo, starting quickly back down the steps. "Time is growing short. Eshku is a desert country, so you must travel by caravan, the ancient way of traveling across Droon's deserts."

"Caravan," sang Quill. "Ah, the romance of a great land voyage. A long ribbon of travelers, weaving its way across the sands."

Neal broke into a smile. "Sounds cool."

"Actually, not so cool," chirped the pen. "It's rather hot in the desert. But not for me, of course. I have a built-in fan!" He waved himself back and forth.

At the bottom of the Tower, Vasa entered a hallway. "And since you will be going into the past, you must have very special rides. *Enchanted* rides. They will take you wherever — and *whenever* — you need to go. But beware. Saba can travel in time, too. He will find you and try to stop you."

Eric didn't like that idea. "But Galen will be there to help us. It'll be just like the old days."

"The very old days," said Bodo.

"And I shall write it all down!" said Quill.

As the city tilted again, they hurried from one chamber to another until they came out into a large courtyard. There they found five blue-haired pilkas with long wavy manes. Larger than the usual white pilkas, they held their heads high and stamped their many feet on the cobblestones. Each had a decorated saddle and bulging saddlebags.

"They're magnificent," said Julie.

Quill hopped from Bodo's hand to the back of one pilka and flicked open its saddlebag. "When in Eshku . . . dress like Eshkuians!"

Keeah looked into one saddlebag and pulled out a bundle of marvelously colored scarves. She laughed. "Caravan clothes!"

The riders found clothes packed just for them. Taking only a moment, they all wrapped themselves in lightweight robes and wound scarves around their heads to protect themselves from the desert's sun and heat.

Eric pulled on a pair of black boots and wound a turban around his head, leaving part of it to dangle down his neck. "I feel like an adventure hero," he said.

Neal laughed. "You look like one, too!" He pulled on a long hooded robe the color of grass. Then he donned a pair of slippers

with curved tips. When he wiggled his toes, Julie smiled.

"They look like genie shoes," she said.

"Call me Zabilac the Magnificent!" Neal said with a laugh. "A genie with no powers!"

Max draped his head in purple cloth. "Vasa, you knew we would go, didn't you?"

"We hoped!" said Vasa, smiling. "Now, if your fashion show is quite over, maybe this would be a good time to tell you that . . . you have only one day in Eshku."

Eric nearly choked. "One day? We only have twenty-four hours to travel five hundred years in the past and back to the present?"

"Oh," said Bodo. "Twenty-four hours?" He glanced up at the clock on the courtyard wall. "Actually, fifteen hours and . . . thirty-eight minutes. Until midnight, to be exact."

"I think I'm going to freak out," mumbled Neal.

"Uh, me first!" said Julie.

Eric's heart thumped hard. "Oh, I'm pretty sure *I'll* be the one telling everybody when to freak out. Until midnight?"

"Collect the five treasures before our diamonds run out at midnight," said Bodo, "or our city will be lost, the stories will be lost, the staircase will be lost, and Droon will be lost. Not to mention the Upper World, too."

Keeah glanced at her friends. "I'm noticing a theme. We'd better get those treasures!"

Eeeeee! The calls of more wingsnakes shattered the air once again. Then came the low rumble of Ko's floating palace.

"Time's up!" said Quill, hopping up to Keeah's saddle with a tiny pack looped around his waist. "I've got my ink. I've got my scroll. Let's go!"

"Good luck in Eshku," said Bodo.

"*Bon voyage,* you voyagers!" added Vasa. "I hear the weather in Eshku is . . . *changeable*!"

As the slithering shadows darkened over the city, the five friends mounted the blue pilkas. At once — *wumpeta-wumpeta!* — the creatures charged down the narrow street and headed straight for the distant wall.

"To Eshku, pilkas!" cried Eric. "As fast as you can. Faster!"

As if on command, the pilkas did run faster. When the swarms of wingsnakes dived at them, the pilkas leaped right at the city wall.

"Oh, no, no!" cried Max, covering his eyes.

But Eric felt the pilkas lifting, lifting, until they cleared the wall altogether — *whooooosh!*

When he looked down, he saw the Kalahar Valley glittering beneath them and fiery snakes circling far below.

"Holy cow!" he gasped. "We're flying!"

The pilkas *were* flying. They sailed higher and higher until the air around them suddenly crackled with blue lightning. Then the pilkas began to fall.

"I'm gonna freak out now!" shouted Neal.

"No, me —" cried Julie.

A moment later, the pilkas burst through the lightning and galloped onto solid ground, spraying waves of sand high in the air.

"We landed!" cried Keeah. "We made it!"

The pilkas rode as fast as the wind,

then slowed and finally stopped on the crest of a dune streaked with pale violet light. Sand hills rolled away as far as the eye could see.

"Oh! The legendary dunes of Eshku," said Quill. "I remember some of the first story!" Bending to his tiny scroll, he sang as he wrote.

The morning sands are violet,
Yet blaze a golden hue at noon.
Blue seas of sand at each sunset
Turn silver from the midnight moon!

"Quill, that's beautiful," said Julie.
"Let's hope I remember more," he said.
"Holy cow," said Eric. "Look at that."
Peering toward the sun, the six friends saw a giant domed creature loping slowly over the distant horizon.

"I can't believe it," said Max. "Is that Tortu? The magical city on the turtle's back?"

They all remembered Tortu as a giant city of many inhabitants built on the back of an enormous turtle. It was said to have roamed across the wastes of Droon for as long as people could recall. But the turtle they saw now had only two or three small buildings on it, and nothing of the high wall they knew would later encircle the city.

"We really must be in the past," said Keeah. "There's hardly anything built there."

As Eric watched the turtle move below the horizon and out of sight, he knew he would never forget the mysterious moving city. His very first adventures with magic had occurred there.

In the beginning, his powers had been wild and uncontrollable. He had even tried to give them back. But Galen had told him he had gained powers "for a greater purpose."

A greater purpose, he thought now, looking at his fingertips. *Well, what's greater than getting the staircase back and saving both worlds?*

"Come on," said Julie. "Caravan, ho!"

"Hey," said Neal. "Next time I get to say that."

Sometimes in single file, sometimes riding abreast, the five friends and one feather pen wove over the hot dunes as the violet hue of the morning slowly turned the sands golden. The soft thud of the pilkas' hooves kept up a steady beat for nearly an hour until they stopped at the base of a massive dune. Near the crest of the dune, the golden sand was streaked with rivers of black.

"I don't like this place," whispered Neal. "Quill, do you know what's on the other side?"

The pen made a sound like a gulp. "I only recall a little. It goes something like . . . this."

Claws will rip and fangs will bite
Within the dragon's dune of night.

"Nice," Neal grumbled. "I had to ask."

"The dragon's dune of night?" said Eric, shivering suddenly. "Do you mean the moon dragon? Is Gethwing here, so long ago? Is this where the first treasure is?"

Keeah looked at him, then at the black sand. "I think there's only one way to find out."

Dismounting, the five friends began to climb the giant wall of streaked sand. What looked at first like a dark bird hovering over the dune turned out to be a ragged banner, waving in the desert wind.

"Bad guys love to advertise," said Julie.

When they peeked over the top, they saw a big black palace shaped like a dragon's head.

"It's got to be Gethwing's palace," said Eric.

The palace's long snout ended in a gate hung with rows of rusted fangs two feet wide.

"Boy, do I wanna go in there," said Neal.

Max grumbled. "That makes none of us —"

"Hush!" said Julie. "Everybody down!"

Two bearlike beasts with shaggy gray fur and blazing eyes came hustling over the far side of the dune and marched right into the dragon's mouth.

Held tight between them was a boy struggling to get free. He seemed only a few years older than the children themselves.

Max squinted at the boy. Then he jumped.

"Oh, my gosh! I can't believe it! That boy! It's . . . Galen!"

Four

The Dragon's Dune of Night

It was Galen. His long brown hair was pushed back behind his ears. He wore a blue tunic and boots and had a short staff tucked into his belt. He squirmed wildly, but the bear-beasts held him fast in their massive paws. When they shouted, the rusty fangs of the gate rose, and the beasts pushed Galen inside.

"Poor Galen," whispered Keeah.

"To see my master after so long," whimpered Max. "And to see him caught!"

"I guess it's good we're here," said Julie.

The young wizard disappeared into the darkness, and the gate slammed shut with a puff of sand and a resounding *thud*.

"Shall we break down the gate now?" asked Max excitedly. "Or now?"

Keeah shook her head. "We'll help him. But we have to be smart about it."

Eric scanned the walls. Two large orbs of red glass gleamed like eyes from what must have been fires inside. The rest of the palace appeared as solid as iron.

"It looks pretty impossible," he mumbled.

"I have one idea," said Neal.

Julie blinked. "Quick, call the newspapers!"

"No, really," said Neal. "Maybe it's the

wiggly genie shoes, but I know how we can get right in. Ten minutes, tops."

Keeah narrowed her eyes at him. "Neal?"

"No, listen," he said. "If we *try* to get inside, the beasts will try to keep us out. Instead . . . we could do what Galen did!"

Max frowned. "Get captured by beasts?"

"Get *pretend* captured by *pretend* beasts," said Neal. He turned to Julie and smiled. "Because one of us can turn herself into a beast just by thinking about it. Isn't that right . . . *Julie*?"

She backed down the dune. "Oh, no. No, no, no, no. I was a beast before. I didn't like it much. Huh-uh. No. And by the way? No."

"Julie," said Keeah, "it *is* a good plan. . . ."

"I like Plan B better," said Julie.

Neal frowned. "Wait. There is no Plan B."

Julie slumped her shoulders. "But a beast? My hair! The smell! My *hair* . . . ohhh . . ."

Five minutes later, a very round beast covered with gray fuzz stood wobbling just below the crest of the dune. It had one big eye in the center of its face. It had no feet, only two pairs of fuzzy flippers.

Julie grunted, turning her single red eye on her friends. "I guess I'm not very good at changing shape."

"Look at it this way," said Eric. "You're both beauty *and* the beast rolled into one. And I do mean *rolled*."

"Very funny," she said. "Somehow, I'm not amused. But come on. We'd better get going."

As Julie rolled up the dune, Quill hopped like a plume into Eric's turban. "Good. I can see everything from here. Come on, people!"

The small band descended the dune, the children marching, Julie rolling herself along the sand behind them with her fuzzy flippers.

When they approached the fanged gate, she growled to the guards. "More humans!"

Errch! The gate rose, and they went inside.

"See what I mean?" Neal whispered as they passed the guards. "We got into the zoo for free!"

"You *hope* it's for free," Keeah whispered. "We still don't know what we'll find in here."

Julie herded the children past the guards. After a few yards, they entered a dark hallway and found themselves alone.

"What I do for Droon!" said Julie, rolling to a stop. "You guys hunt for the first treasure. I suppose it's easier to find Galen like this."

"Good call," said Eric. "If all goes well, you can get us and Galen out the same way. Julie, you're the best beast ever!"

"Yeah, yeah," she mumbled as she rolled away, bounced into a wall, then turned right.

The kids crept left into a narrow passage, dashed to the next corner, and flattened themselves against the wall.

"Wait," said Quill. "I remember something." He peeked around the corner from Eric's turban, then jumped back. "I knew it. Gethwing. The dragon. He's coming!"

"Yikes!" said Neal. "In here —"

They rushed into the nearest opening and found themselves in a large candlelit room with a gallery running around the top. At the far end of the room stood a big throne with cutouts on the back as if it was made for a creature with wings.

"Good one," groaned Eric. "Gethwing's living room."

"Everyone, upstairs!" said Keeah. "Hurry!"

They raced up a narrow set of stairs to the gallery and crouched behind a railing just as Gethwing entered. The dragon strode quietly to the center of the room. He glanced around quickly, then turned to the door, his long spiky tail swaying slowly across the floor.

"Blegg," he said. "Come . . ."

"We need to go!" whispered Max.

"No, wait," said Eric. "I have to know what he's got up his scaly sleeve. Two minutes —"

Eric crept along the gallery until he was over the center of the room. He stopped behind a post in the railing and peeked around.

Shh-lump! Shh-lump! A small gray creature with knobby skin and a large head limped into the room.

Quill leaned forward, his scroll open.

The beast bowed, then seemed to have trouble raising its heavy head again. "Blegg, master thief, reporting, Emperor Geffwink!"

The moon dragon eyed the beast coldly. "No, no, Blegg. Ko is still the ruler of the beasts. For now, at least —"

"Holy cow," whispered Eric. "Gethwing wants to be emperor!"

"But tell me," the dragon said, "did you find the treasure to help me on my quest?"

The little beast grinned, showing two big teeth and no more. "The Talos is in the Chamber of Fear, awaiting your instructions."

"The Talos," whispered Keeah. "That must be our first treasure. Let's go find it."

"No, wait!" said Eric. "What quest is Gethwing going on? We need to know —"

But Neal, Max, and Keeah were already creeping back down the gallery to the stairs.

Quill stayed with Eric. "I'd go myself," he whispered. "But I must write it all down!"

"Thanks," said Eric. He watched Keeah pause at the top of the stairs, turn to him one last time, and mouth the word "Now!"

He shook his head and she quietly descended the stairs with Neal and Max. They slipped out of the room together.

"Maybe we should go, too," said Eric.

Suddenly, Gethwing spoke again.

"The prophecy says that a boy shall find it. Well, I ask you, Blegg, what boy *is* there but him? Little boy. Little baby. Little . . . Sparr!"

It was all Eric could do not to yell. "Quill! Gethwing must want Sparr to help him on his quest. That's why he followed Sparr to the Upper World!"

"But we're deep in the past," whispered Quill. "Gethwing and Sparr are in your world *now*."

Eric thought about that. "Okay, but what if Gethwing never got his chance? What if Ko put him and all the beasts to sleep before Gethwing got to the Upper World with Sparr? But now that Sparr is a boy again, and Gethwing's awake, he finally has his chance."

Quill made a sound like a gulp. "Then I'd say we're all in trouble."

"The boy will show me where it is," said the dragon. "Oh, the power of the thing —"

Errch! A distant heavy squeak meant that the front gate was being hoisted up.

"What thing?" hissed Eric. "Come on, you fangy monster! You chased Sparr into my world to get something. What is it?"

A sudden commotion among the guards was followed by the loud tread of footsteps echoing in the hallways.

Quill and Eric looked at each other.

"Uh-oh!" said the pen. "The phantom? Is he here? Is Saba already here?"

Gethwing spun on his heels and faced the door. "If it's Ko, he will take the Talos!"

"But what about Emperor Geffwink?" asked Blegg. "Your plans to rule Droon —"

The doorway was suddenly filled with the shape of an armor-wearing beast with a bull's head. Blegg flattened completely to the floor, and Gethwing bowed.

"Ko!" boomed the moon dragon. "I didn't expect you in my house, great Emperor —"

Only it wasn't the emperor. The creature at the door cast no shadow.

"Where is it?" roared the phantom. "Where is the Talos?" His voice sounded to Eric like thunder in a tunnel.

Still bowing, Gethwing replied, "The Talos? Why, it's in the Chamber of Fear waiting for you. I had one of my beasts steal it for you!"

Saba scanned the room slowly. He was about to turn away, when he raised his twin-horned head toward the gallery. His three eyes blazed when he spotted Eric.

"A boy!" Saba roared.

Gethwing raised his head now and saw Eric, too. "A . . . boy?"

"Uh, sorry. Time to go!" cried Eric. Grabbing Quill, he leaped over the railing, landed on the floor, and shot out of the room before either Saba or Gethwing could make a move.

He ran as fast as his legs could carry him. "Quill!" he gasped. "Please tell me this story has a happy ending!"

The sound of yelling and the stomping of feet echoed close behind them.

"Sorry!" said Quill as they ran. "We're making it up as we go!"

Eric slid around the corner seconds ahead of the roaring phantom and the moon dragon. "Oh, well, I had to ask!"

Five

The First Wizard

Eric raced down one hall after another, his desert robes flying. Quill was busy trying not to fall out of his turban. "This is shaping up to be a great story!" he squeaked.

"I hope it gets better than this!" cried Eric.

"I doubt it will," said Quill. "We're going to the Chamber of Fear, remember — left now!"

When they shot left into a narrow passage, Eric glimpsed Saba's horns blasting black fire behind him.

"Arrrh!" the phantom roared.

At the end of the passage was a steep spiral staircase. Eric leaped down the stairs and wound around and around until he jumped off the last one onto the ground.

"Okay, now which way —"

"In here!" said a voice.

A fuzzy gray flipper jerked out of the shadows and pulled Eric into a tiny dark space.

"Julie!" said Eric.

"Hush! Here he comes!" she said.

The phantom thudded down the spiral staircase and paused for a second. A moment later, he stormed away to another part of the dragon's palace.

"Thanks for the save!" sighed Quill.

Whoosh! A spark lit up the tiny room, and Eric saw Keeah, Max, and Neal huddling next to Julie. Keeah's fingertips blazed with sparks.

"Awesome, you guys," he said. "Thanks."

"And for the best part, look!" said Max.

They moved aside to show two bear-like beasts bound up in spider-silk ropes. Standing over them was a young boy in a blue cloak, a pile of loose chains around his feet. He grinned at Eric.

"Galen!" Eric exclaimed. "That's even awesomer!"

"I think so, too," said the young wizard.

The kids had seen young Galen only once before. It was when they had traveled up Ko's Dark Stair to the Upper World and found themselves in the year 1470. At that time, Galen was almost exactly their age.

"Your friends told me everything about

the future," the young wizard said to Eric. "I still can't believe the staircase is gone."

"The Guardians are sure that if we find the treasures, we can bring it back," said Julie. "If the Talos is the first treasure, it's in the Chamber of Fear."

Galen nodded, then peeked out of the room and looked both ways. "The Talos belongs to an ancient people called the *droomar*," he said. "They've kept magic and wisdom alive in the dark time of the beasts."

"I'm a *droomar*!" said Keeah proudly. "Well, I become one in the future."

Galen smiled. "Good. I'm beginning to think that Droon needs all the help it can get."

"What does the Talos do?" asked Max.

"It shows what's happening in the heavens," said the young wizard. "The stars, the moon, everything."

"Well, Gethwing had it stolen for some quest," said Eric. "Now, back in our time, he and Sparr are in the Upper World."

Galen frowned. "Let's find the Talos and get those stairs back. By the way, the Chamber of Fear is what beasts call the kitchen —"

"The kitchen?" said Neal. "Stand aside for the kitchen expert. I'll nose it out!"

With that, Neal shot out of the room and jumped back up the spiral stairs, taking two steps at a time.

Eric blinked at his friends. "Things sure do move quickly around here."

"Especially us," said Keeah. "Let's go!"

Julie twirled quickly, and she became herself again. "Next time, Plan B. I really mean it."

"And Plan B is . . . we run!" said Max.

At the top of the stairs, Neal led them

away from the beasts and into a tangle of narrow passages and rooms.

With every step, Eric was becoming more and more convinced that the reason Gethwing chased Sparr into the Upper World was because of his quest to find something.

The sooner we get the staircase back, he thought, *the sooner we'll know.*

Neal darted down a hall, up a short set of stairs, paused, turned, and suddenly held up his hand. "Hear that?"

Shink! Shink!

"I know that sound," he whispered.

Sidling up to a door, the friends peeked in and saw two snail-like beasts huddled over a big stove. They were using long daggers to scrape chopped vegetables into a giant steaming pot.

The room was bathed in red light. Looking up, Eric saw that the ceiling above them had a large round red window. He knew at once that it was one of the palace's dragon eyes.

"There it is," said Keeah.

On a table across the room were a bowl, a spoon, a pair of twisted spectacles, and a short golden cylinder dotted with green jewels.

Galen stared at the table. "The Talos. Now, how to get to it without the snails seeing us?"

"And get out again, too," said Max.

Neal chuckled softly. "I wonder . . ."

"I won't do it!" hissed Julie.

"No, I'm thinking of a little distraction," said Neal. "And I think I can . . . wait . . ." He pulled his hood low, puffed up his robes, and leaned over. "There —"

"Neal, what are you thinking?" said Eric.

"I'm not thinking," he said. "I'm doing!"

Looking like a large old man, Neal

waddled slowly into the room. "You there, kitchen beasts!" he said in as low a voice as possible.

The giant snails turned and stared at him.

"Huh?" said one, raising its dagger.

"I am Zabilac the Magnificent, the new cook for Emperor Ko!" said Neal. "Gethwing sent me to get your recipe for" — he sniffed the big pot — "beastie soup!"

The beasts looked at each other.

"Okay," said the second one. "First you start with garlic. . . ."

"Neal is perfectly fearless!" whispered Quill. "And it makes for a great story!"

While Neal huddled closely with the snails, the others slipped silently over to the table. Eric reached up and pulled down the golden shaft. It was about a foot long and covered with sparkling jewels.

"It's really beautiful," said Julie. "What does it do?"

Galen smiled. "It makes a little shoosh-ing noise when you shake it. Blegg must be in a beastie band. This," he said, picking up the twisted pair of spectacles, "is the Talos."

Keeah peered through the glasses, then pulled her head back. "They're blurry! And they hurt!"

The wizard smiled. "They're very old. Maybe if you buff them up —"

Suddenly, the kitchen doorway was filled by a dark, shadowless figure.

"Uh-oh, it's him again!" chittered Max.

The phantom's three red eyes burned when he spotted the children. "Beasts, be gone!" he boomed. "Children, give me the Talos!"

Surprised, the beasts slithered away from the boiling pot and out the door. With a swift move, Saba bolted it behind them.

"I don't like that," said Galen.

Saba stepped slowly toward the children.

"Guys!" whispered Neal, pulling everyone back with him toward the stove, "this soup is really hot. We could spill it and . . . and . . ."

"Climb out the eye," said Eric, looking up.

Max's paws began to move. "I'll make a rope —"

"Give me the Talos!" Saba thundered again. He took another step toward them.

"Now!" cried Keeah. "Off the floor!"

In a flash, everyone jumped to the counter.

Eric, Julie, and Neal kicked over the giant pot. It splashed down to the floor just as Max tossed his spider-silk rope to the ceiling.

"Ahhh!" yelled Saba as the soup washed around his feet. He jumped back to the door.

The kids leaped to the rope, pulled it down, and — *boing!* — it bounced them right up to the red eye in the ceiling.

Up, up, up they went until — *crash!* — they burst through the window and clambered out onto the cheek of the dragon's head.

But no sooner had they escaped than blue lightning began to crash and crackle over the golden sands, and the pilkas raced around the top of the dune, whinnying loudly.

"It's time for the next story," said Quill.

"Arrrh!" Saba appeared in the window. He wasn't far behind them.

Suddenly, Gethwing and his beasts burst out of the gates and began to climb up over the dragon's chin. The kids were surrounded!

Galen frowned. "All in all, getting in was so much easier —"

"I have an idea," said Neal, looking up.

"Three in one day?" asked Max.

Neal smiled. "It really must be the slippers. I'm thinking it's time to lower the flag."

Julie looked at him. "Lower the flag?"

"Pole," said Neal. "Lower the flag*pole*. If we knock it over, it'll be a bridge to the pilkas!"

As Saba's horns burst through the window, and the beasts charged up the dragon's snout, the six friends pushed the flagpole back and forth until — *ka-foom!* — it crashed like a falling tree onto the surrounding dune.

"Time to run!" said Julie. "Let's go!"

Saba roared and the beasts howled as the kids scurried across the pole to the sands. The pilkas raced straight to them.

"Great escape, Neal," said Galen, handing him the spectacles. "Since the first time I set foot in Droon, I knew this place was magical. You've just proved it again. Good luck, friends!"

As the kids, Max, and Quill jumped on the pilkas, Galen dashed away between the dunes and was gone.

"Onward!" said Max. "To our next stop in Eshku!"

"Caravan, ho!" yelled Neal.

As Saba charged across the dunes after them, and the beasts followed close behind, the pilkas galloped directly into the storm.

Dark winds and swirling sand engulfed them completely, and still the pilkas raced faster and deeper into the storm.

All of a sudden, the winds ceased to blow, the darkness vanished, and the voyagers galloped out into a valley of golden sand.

"We did it!" cheered Julie. "We made it into the second story!"

Suddenly — *thwank-thwank-thwank!* — a ring of flaming arrows struck the sand all around the little caravan, trapping them in a blazing cage of fire.

"I think we made it into something else, too!" said Keeah.

All at once, the dunes ran red with the shape of plump, angry warriors.

"Ninns!" cried Max. "We've been captured by Ninns!"

Six

Song of the Ninns

Keeah and Eric didn't even have time to send out a quick spray of sparks, and Neal could barely stuff the Talos in his robe before the Ninns had forced the whole band from their pilkas.

The fight was over before it began.

Whinnying loudly, the pilkas reared, then galloped off into the distance in a flash.

Eric sighed. "They really are fast. Too bad we're not on them."

"For the record," said Neal, "this time being captured was *not* my idea."

"Hoo-hoo!" cheered the Ninns. They beat their armor with their fists. Then they marched the children and Max, with Quill still in Eric's turban, back up the dune in single file.

When they reached the top, the children gasped. Spread out across the open sand below them was a vast number of red tents. Paths and alleys crisscrossed and curved among them. Colorful flags and banners curled from every one, snapping musically in the hot breeze.

"A Ninn city," said Julie.

"It looks like thousands of them here," said Keeah. "I wonder if they're on a mission for Ko."

Quill leaned down from Eric's turban. His feathers twitched. "Ko, perhaps. But we must be something like a hundred years later than last time. Look!"

He motioned into the distance. Crawling slowly over the distant sands was the giant turtle again, its short tail curled high. But the city on Tortu's back was larger this time. A blue wall, eight feet tall in some places, circled the buildings. Three towers twisted up from the center of the turtle's dome.

"It's later in Droon's history," said Keeah.

"Later in the day, too," said Eric, looking up. "Maybe three o'clock. Nine hours left."

Neal frowned. "And four treasures to go."

"And four Galens," said Max.

No sooner had they started down into the tent city than the warriors pointed up at a dark shape streaking across the sun.

"Dragon ship!" shouted a Ninn.

"Ko is coming!" cried another. "Our leader!"

Eric turned to Keeah. "The Ninns are looking for the dragon ship. This is amazing. It must be four hundred years ago."

They all knew the story of how, long ago, Ko was near death and fled on a dragon-shaped airship, charming himself to sleep for four centuries. It was when Ko woke that Sparr became a child again.

"If a century has passed since our last stop," Quill whispered, "then Ko has just gone to sleep. The Ninns don't know it, but they have been left all alone!"

The dark shape was not the dragon ship. It was only a cloud drifting across the sun. Blown about by the wind, the cloud dissolved and passed away into nothing.

The Ninns looked for a moment longer, then lowered their heads, grunted, and marched into the tent city. They pushed the children into a tent and used a stout rope to tie them to a thick post in the center.

"You wait!" grunted one of the Ninns.

"For what, exactly?" asked Keeah.

"You see what!" the Ninn gargled.

The warriors slouched through the flap and were gone. The one who had spotted the cloud on the sun stood guard outside.

The tent had a bed, a small table, a wide chair, and a smoldering fire on which something was slowly cooking.

"I was in a Ninn tent once before," said Eric, twisting his hands. "A kind Ninn lady let me go. I guess it would be pretty impossible for that to happen again."

"While we're waiting for the impossible," said Neal, "how about you and Keeah blast yourselves free, then untie us?"

Keeah wiggled her hands and tried to point her fingers. She shook her head. "It's too tight. I can't get a good aim."

Eric tried the same thing. "My hands

are too close together. If I tried to free you, I'd probably blow myself up."

Neal frowned. "But I'd be free, right?"

Eric just glared at him.

Julie tried to wiggle out of her ropes, too, but only got herself more tangled. Quill nearly bent his tip trying to untie Max's bonds.

"This is hopeless!" said the spider troll.

"Wait. I hear a voice," said Quill.

"If it's Galen, maybe he can free *us* this time," said Neal.

"I hear it, too," said Julie. "But it's not Galen. It's someone . . . singing."

From just outside the tent came the sound of a little voice singing softly.

Tortu roams from dune to dune,
Crisscrossing every inch of Droon.
And like the wandering turtle dome,
We Ninns are searching for our home.

With each beat of the song came a playful splashing sound like the tinkling of bells.

A moment later, the tent cloth quivered, and a small Ninn girl in a purple dress wiggled under it. She had big red cheeks, and her wispy brown hair was tied into pigtails. She held out a short stick covered with metal rings.

"I'm Theesha. Do you want to play?" She shook the stick. *Shing-a-ling!*

Eric smiled. "Sorry, we can't. Our hands are tied up —"

"I can free you!" she said.

"Maybe you shouldn't," said Keeah. "You'll get in trouble with the warrior outside."

The girl peeked out the flap of the tent. When she pulled her head back in, her nose was wrinkled in laughter. "That's no warrior. That's my father! Hey, Minky, come in!"

From the back of the tent came tiny snuffling and snarling sounds. A moment later, a young groggle the size of a small puppy loped under the tent and came to the children.

"Chew, Minky!" said the Ninn girl.

Making a happy little purring sound, the groggle chewed the kids' bonds one by one.

"Thank you, Theesha," said Keeah, rubbing her wrists. "Now we really need to be going. We need to find something. You haven't seen any treasures around here, have you?"

The girl frowned. "We don't have any-thing like that," she said. Then she brightened. "But you can have my ripple stick! Really." She handed it to Keeah.

"Thank you," said the princess. She shook it once, then slipped it under her belt.

"Something is happening," said Max.

"Come this way," said Theesha. "Maybe you can find the treasure!"

Pulling Keeah by the hand, she slipped out the back of the tent and trotted quickly down a narrow alley between two rows of tents. The children and Max followed. When she got to the end of the alley, Theesha stopped and crouched behind one big tent.

Looking around, the kids saw that all the red warriors had gathered and were looking up.

"He comes! He comes!" they shouted.

"Not Ko, I hope," whispered Eric. "That's impossible."

Another dark shadow crossed the sun, but it was neither a cloud nor Ko's dragon ship. It was a jet-black balloon with tattered banners and ribbons flying about it. But more frightening than the balloon itself was the young man standing inside its basket.

He was a teenager dressed all in black. He wore a long cloak with a high collar and a helmet of spikes down the middle of his head. A set of dark fins grew behind his ears.

"Holy crow," gasped Julie. "It's Sparr —"

The balloon slowed overhead.

Eric recognized Sparr's face. But there was something strange in his eyes. He was older than the boy they had come to know in the present, and he had changed. His look was narrow and shifty, his brow was low, and his lips were hard and cruel.

He's already begun to turn evil, thought Eric.

"Ninns!" Sparr yelled out, leaping to the rim of the basket. He held the ropes and stared down at the gathered warriors.

The Ninns looked back but said nothing.

"I have some good news and bad news!" Sparr announced. "First the bad news. Look for Ko no more! He has flown away on his dragon ship and will not return!"

Neal snorted. "Until you bring him back!"

Keeah shook her head. "We're at the exact time that Sparr began his life of evil."

"And now the good news!" the boy said, swinging on the ropes. "I am your new chief, your commander, your leader. Allow me to introduce myself. I am . . . Lord Sparr! You will follow this symbol!"

The sorcerer then unfurled a large banner on the side of the balloon's basket. On the banner was the old Droon symbol for Sparr's name: an upside-down triangle with a lightning bolt running through it. The lightning bolt meant that Sparr was a son of Zara.

"I'll get my stuff labeled when I go bad, too," whispered Neal. "It's the thing to do."

"As a sign of my magical ability, I have built a palace of power," Sparr boomed as the balloon began to rise again.

Julie shook her head. "What's with bad guys and palaces?" she said. "Why can't they just live in regular houses?"

"In my palace are amazing new treasures to help us conquer Droon!" shouted Sparr.

"Treasures!" said Eric.

"And I have already captured my biggest enemy —"

"Galen!" whispered Max. "He's captured Galen, and he has the treasure!"

"Join me at my Rose Palace," Sparr said finally as the balloon rose even higher. "And we shall take over Droon. Follow me — now!"

"We will!" Eric whispered.

Suddenly, Quill jumped. "Oh! I see Saba!"

The kids turned to see a plume of dust rising from the distant dunes. But it wasn't coming toward them. Saba was racing across the open sand and away from them.

The sorcerer's balloon flew up, and the Ninns hustled back to their tents to pack.

"Sparr's heading for his palace," said Keeah. "Saba must be going there, too. Guys, we have to get there before any of them —"

"I know how!" said Theesha. "Minky has a mommy!" She whistled and — *flap-flap!* — a large groggle swooped down to them.

"Go, find your treasure!" said Theesha.

Keeah hugged the Ninn girl. "Thank you for everything. We'll always remember you."

In a flash the kids, spider troll, and feather pen climbed onto the groggle's back.

"Groggle," said Max, "follow that balloon!"

A moment later, the flying lizard lifted away and chased Sparr's black balloon as it rose higher, higher, and higher over the golden desert below.

Seven

The Luck of the Voyagers

"We're losing Sparr!" said Max, sitting between Julie and Eric on the groggle's back.

"Go, Minky's mom," urged Neal.

"But stay hidden," added Keeah. "We need to find the palace, but we can't let Sparr see us."

With a powerful flap of its wings, the groggle swept under the balloon, following its course.

They flew farther and farther from the

tent city. Finally, just as they drifted over one large dune, the kids saw Sparr's palace looming up before them. Built of rose-colored stone, it had many levels of fountains, courtyards, columns, ramps, and hanging gardens from the ground all the way up to its pointed summit.

"It's beautiful," said Quill.

"It's beautiful . . . and it's mine!" cried Sparr. "But who are you and where did you come from?"

Startled, the kids looked up to see the sorcerer glaring down at them.

"Uh . . . the future," said Neal.

"The future?" said Sparr. "Well, it's never too early to teach you a lesson. Take this!"

Ka-blam! He hurled a bolt of jagged red light. Minky's mother arched back suddenly to avoid the blast, and before they could stop themselves, the children fell off.

Luckily, they were close to the top of the

palace. They splashed down into the uppermost fountain and slid down to the next level and the next and the next until they rolled — soaking wet but safe — onto the main level.

Jumping to their feet, they saw the groggle peck at Sparr. His balloon spun out of control, slammed into the palace, then crashed and rolled down every terrace all the way to the ground.

"Ouch," said Neal. "That'll leave a mark."

"Uh-oh, people," said Julie. "We have company. Look."

She pointed three dunes away to where the phantom was running hard and getting closer. "Saba will be here in minutes!"

"Let's get inside the palace," said Keeah. "To Galen! And the second treasure!"

The children hurried under an archway dangling with vines and into a maze of columns and ramps and arches. Sunlight

shafted down from open ceilings, creating shadows even in the brightest spaces.

Suddenly, they stopped.

In the middle of the maze was a statue of a young man with a faint beard, wearing a tunic and boots and holding out a curved staff with both hands as if he were defending himself.

"Oh!" said Max, running to the statue. "My master. My poor, frozen master!"

"Sparr must have cast a spell on him," said Neal. He touched the wizard's staff. "He's frozen solid."

Keeah leaned over the base of the statue and traced several strange markings written on it. "There's an old spell around the base. But it's in a very odd language."

Eric looked at the symbols. On their last adventure he had seen strange characters in an ancient language, and from somewhere deep inside of him had come the sound and sense of those old words. They came to him again.

"I can read it," he said.

"Are you kidding?" said Neal. "Awesome!"

"Eric," said Keeah. "You really have to tell us how you know."

"I don't know how I know," he said. "I just do."

Pulling in a deep breath, he spoke. The words sounded like whisperings in a tunnel.

A sudden shower of blue raindrops jangled and tinkled as they fell around the wizard. There was a sharp cracking sound — *kkk!* — and then the statue moved.

"Yeowww!" said Galen. He stretched and wiggled. Then he laughed and hopped down to the ground. "Well, that was not fun —"

"Also not fun is — me!" snarled a voice.

They turned around and Sparr was there again, standing in the maze of columns.

He was soaking wet.

"Thanks for nearly wrecking my balloon, kiddies!" he said, his eyes narrowing.

With one swift move, Galen jumped in front of the kids. "The treasure must be deep in the palace. I'll take care of this guy!"

Raising his curved staff, he swung it around in the air until it made a humming sound. "So, Sparr. I've had my rest. Wanna play?"

Sparr drew a jagged saber from his belt and lunged at the wizard. "It *will* be play, beating you! Shouldn't you retire, old man?"

"I'm not much older than you," said Galen. "Where I come from, that's called *experience*!"

Clack! Blang! The two brothers charged at each other, racing around the courtyard, then leaping to a ramp and fighting their way up to the next level. With every step and jump, their weapons clashed and clattered.

"Go!" shouted Galen. "Saba's almost here!"

The children, Max, and Quill raced into the depths of the palace. Soon, the desert light faded into shadows. There were strange noises, creakings, flutterings, and mysterious echoes. All the while, the passages grew narrower and colder.

Quill trembled in Eric's turban. "As bright as it was outside, it's spooky inside the palace. The very air oozes dark power."

"My thoughts exactly," said Neal. "Like Sparr himself."

They stopped finally at a giant black door.

"I'm afraid," said Max.

"We should go in anyway," said Eric. "The treasure is probably right in there."

Everyone nodded. But nobody moved.

"I'm not going in first," said Eric. "I just said we *should* go in."

"Don't look at me," said Neal, wiggling his shoes. "I have no powers. I'm just colorful."

"And I'm all done being a beastie," said Julie. "Besides, I never fly inside."

Quill began to whistle softly. So did Max.

Keeah sighed. "What a bunch of heroes we are. All right, I'll lead. But don't crowd me. I'll need room to run if things get too scary."

Taking the lead, the princess pushed open the black door. Inside was a large domed chamber. A fire burned in a hole in the center.

"What *is* this place?" asked Julie.

"A real Chamber of Fear?" said Neal.

Looking around, Eric guessed what it was. "Sparr's workshop. Where he makes things."

Quill scribbled something noisily, then stopped with a gasp. "Like those things?"

On a low anvil, amid hammers and bellows and surrounded by urns of water, sat three objects. One was a large red jewel that shed a dull crimson light. The second was a piece of gold jewelry in the shape of a wasp. The third object was a crown shaped like a snake, coiled upon itself. Its head stood entwined with its tail as if ready to strike.

"The Three Powers!" said Keeah. "The Red Eye of Dawn, the Golden Wasp, and the Coiled Viper. We've come to the exact time that Sparr invented them!"

The Three Powers.

Since their very first visit to Droon, the

friends had been trying to keep Sparr from rediscovering his lost magical objects.

The Red Eye controlled the forces of nature.

The Golden Wasp stung its enemies and turned them into wraiths for Sparr.

And the most powerful of the three, the Coiled Viper, controlled the flow of time. It was the Viper that woke Ko from his long sleep and turned Sparr into a boy again.

"Wait," said Neal. "Are these the treasures we want? Did we find three all at once?"

Keeah frowned. "They can't be. They're evil. Besides, there are three of them."

"We should destroy them," said Max. "Without the Viper, Ko would still be asleep."

"Right," said Eric.

But he also remembered that young Sparr would never exist if it weren't for the

Viper. And as long as young Sparr was on their side, there was a chance that everything in Droon could change for the better.

Keeah picked up the Golden Wasp. It lay in her palm, silent and still. "If this hadn't stung Sparr, I might never have found my mother."

"And if not for the power of the Red Eye of Dawn, Demither the Sea Witch might still be the sorcerer's servant," added Julie.

Eric stared at all three objects. "Maybe some things can't be changed, no matter how bad they are, because good things come from them."

The children were quiet for a while.

"Then Galen can't destroy them either," said Max. "He must do what we know he *did* do. He must hide them."

At that moment, Galen himself charged

into the innermost chamber. "Some palace Sparr built. He's lost in one of his own mazes —"

He stopped. Seeing the Three Powers, he frowned. "Those are evil. We should destroy them now."

"Except that . . . we can't," said Julie.

They quickly explained why the Powers needed to stay in history.

"Charm the Powers into different shapes," said Quill. "Then toss them to the winds! It's one of Droon's greatest legends."

Galen blinked. "Really? Well, I do like legends. Bring them and follow me!"

The friends hustled back through the passages and out to the uppermost terrace of the palace. The sun was beginning to fall in the sky. The vast ocean of sand was tinged with streaks of blue shadow.

Galen set down his staff, then began to

utter words under his breath. Seconds later, the red jewel transformed itself into a small brown pouch. Grinning, the wizard threw it miles through the air until it could be seen no more.

Eric noticed that the phantom was nowhere to be seen. "I think we'd better hurry."

"Okay, then," said Galen. "Let's see how far I can throw this guy." Whispering more words, he turned the Wasp into a gnarly stick. Then he whirled it fast around his head and let go. *Wham!* It slammed into a nearby wall and bounced to the floor. *Zzzzt!*

"That's gonna make him mad," said Neal.

"Sorry!" Galen spun the stick fast again and it shot into the distance like a rocket.

At last, he stared hard at the golden crown.

"How about sending it to the bottom of the Sea of Droon?" suggested Keeah.

Galen grinned. "Perfect." He turned the gleaming Viper into a dull brown rock and hurled it across the sand with all his might. Cupping his ear, he listened. "All gone —"

Suddenly, the sky darkened. It swirled with blue light. In the distance, the enchanted pilkas were racing away to the gathering storm.

"There are the pilkas. And they're leaving without us!" said Max.

"But we have no treasure," said Keeah. "We can't leave —"

"And you won't!" roared a voice.

All at once, Saba the phantom was upon them. He leaped up to the terrace from the level below, his horns spitting black sparks.

"Back off, ugly," said Galen, his fingers already sparking.

"We don't have any treasure," said Julie. "Leave us alone!"

"Let's get out of here," said Quill.

"To the balloon," said Neal. "It's the fastest way." They ran to the edge of the palace, grabbed thick vines, and swung to the ground, plopping down next to Sparr's mangled balloon.

But before they could escape, Saba jumped off the top of the palace and landed next to them. He lunged at Keeah, ripping at her belt. The musical stick Theesha had given her tumbled to the ground.

"Saba's after Theesha's stick," said Eric. "That must be the treasure!"

Saba reached for the stick, but Max dived, grabbed it, and ran back to the princess.

"He wants a stick?" snapped Galen. "I'll give him a stick!"

He whirled his staff in the air. It shed jagged sparks over the phantom. Saba howled.

"Get going!" cried the wizard. "I'll keep him busy while you escape. See you soon!"

"Count on it!" said Keeah.

Scrambling into Sparr's black balloon, the five friends and Quill lifted off.

With a powerful wind, they were swept up once again into the storm of blue lightning.

Eight

The Rat-faced Snitchers of Zoop

The children clung tightly to the balloon ropes as lightning zigzagged all around them.

Then, just as the storm was about to clear, a last jagged bolt of light struck the balloon and sent it sinking fast to the earth.

"We've sprung a leak!" chattered Max. "We're — doomed!"

As they plummeted like stones, a voice

boomed suddenly outside the balloon. "Ho-ho there! Do you folks need a lift?"

An instant later, a large shallow bowl shot up next to them. Sitting in it was a giant man in giant armor. He had a big red nose and a craggy beard. Next to him were two other armored men floating in their own big bowls.

"Old Rolf!" shouted Julie. "Smee? Lunk? The Knights of Silversnow!"

"Humf! If anyone else rides their shields around, I'd like to know about it!" boomed the knight named Rolf.

"Get on board," said the one called Lunk, squinting through the eyeholes in his helmet. "You can land safely, or you can land fast!"

"Out of the basket and into the soup bowl!" added Smee.

Without another word, the kids and

Max leaped from the crashing balloon to the knights' shields just as the balloon collapsed completely.

Crash! It fell to earth like a wet dish towel.

"Sparr's going to be mad about this," said Neal.

Rolf laughed heartily. "Add it to the list!"

The knights were a trio of ancient, oversized battlers who lived in a castle high atop the Ice Hills of Tarabat. They slept a lot, but whenever Galen needed them, they always came to help.

"We're off to find Galen," said Smee with a yawn. He leaned right, banking his shield in a wide circle. Max and Neal leaned with him. "But tell me. We sleep so much that sometimes we don't remember. Have we met before?"

"Sort of," said Keeah. "We meet in the future. But I don't know if you remember us then. Right now, we're traveling back in time."

Rolf laughed again. "Why not? This is Droon, isn't it? Anything is possible!"

"Galen just called us," said Lunk, shifting to make more room for Julie and Eric. "We don't mind. Knights are supposed to help."

"We need to find him, too," said Eric as the shields dipped lower over the blue-hued sand. "The magical staircase disappeared, and to bring it back we have to find some treasures that were stolen in our time."

"And wherever Galen is," said Julie, "is the next treasure."

"Then, let's make tracks," said Old Rolf. "To the Rat-faced Snitchers of Zoop!"

Quill squeaked. "I remember them. They gave their name to this very story!"

Whooosh! The knights drove their shields faster into the late afternoon sky, skimming the desert sands. The pilkas raced below.

It wasn't long before Rolf slowed at an oasis of palm trees waving around a glittering pool.

The knights silently steered the shields into the tallest tree and stopped, completely hidden in its bushy cluster of leaves.

"Well, look at that," said Lunk, squinting down. "If it isn't sand ponies. And Snitchers!"

The children carefully parted the leaves and looked down. A herd of small horses trotted over a nearby dune and into the oasis. Sitting on the ponies were little creatures with big heads. They had narrow, whiskered snouts and puffy purple pants.

"They look like eggplants," Julie said softly.

"I like eggplants," said Lunk, getting a faraway look in his eyes.

"Nobody likes *them*, though," said Smee. "Sneaking Snitchers. They love to steal."

"So does Saba," said Keeah.

The purple-panted creatures dismounted and gathered at the blue pool. One of them, who had bright yellow hair and seemed to be their leader, dug into his saddlebag and pulled out something hidden under a cloth.

"Snitchers!" he announced. "Long and hard have we ridden. Our prize have we snitched!"

He removed the cloth.

The creatures cheered. "Snitch! Snitch!"

"Is it the treasure?" asked Julie, squinting between the large palm leaves. "I can't see."

Neal craned his neck. "I don't think so. It looks like a cheese Danish —"

Max gasped. "No . . . it can't be. . . ."

He dangled from the tree for a closer look. "It is!" he hissed, scrambling back up again. "Robbers! Thieves! Stealers! Takers!"

"Snitchers?" whispered Lunk.

"Snitchers!" Max growled. "They must bury that back in the ground where they found it!"

Eric turned to Max. "Back in the ground? What do you mean?"

The spider troll trembled. "They have stolen the one and only gizzleberry seed! It's the most precious possession of my people!"

Placing his hands on his hips, the chief Snitcher yelled, "Bring Smash, son of Thud!"

When he saw another baggy-panted Snitcher bring a giant hammer from his saddlebag, Max nearly jumped out of the tree. "A hammer! They'll kill the seed!"

"Is it a special seed?" asked Neal.

"Special?" gasped Max. "It is said that this seed contains the secret of life itself! If you plant the gizzleberry seed — *zip!* — trees with every variety of berry grow instantly. The purple, of course, but also the rose and the yellow and the ruby and the pungent green. Not to mention the sapphire-blue berries so often used as breakfast toppings!"

"In short," said Rolf, "if they destroy that seed, Droon as we know it shall come to a very bitter end!"

"Then that's the treasure," said Eric.

Neal blew out a slow breath. "So the future of Droon isn't only in the deserts of the past, it's also in the *desserts* of the past!"

Quill scribbled that down. "Tastily put, Neal."

"We have to get the seed," said Max firmly.

As the chief Snitcher placed the seed

squarely on a rock, Rolf pointed. "It looks like someone already tried and failed."

Draped over the saddle of one small pony was someone nearly completely hidden in a sack. Only a pair of blue boots stuck out.

"Galen!" said Julie.

"Huh," mumbled Neal. "Did you ever notice that he seems to get caught a lot?"

"I guess that's why we're here," said Lunk.

"Luckily, Galen gave us a spell," said Rolf. "It'll free him instantly. Smee, if you please!"

As the Snitchers huddled around the hammer below, Smee produced a tiny scroll. It unrolled to a length of about three feet.

"I don't know about *instantly*," he said. "There's awfully small writing here. . . ."

"Oh, please hurry!" urged Max.

While the Snitchers giggled and danced around the seed, the knights began to read.

"Punky . . . lunky . . . floo . . ."

"A little for each of us!" said the chief, as his fellow Snitcher raised the big hammer called Smash higher and higher.

". . . mello . . . padooba . . . kemlem . . ."

"We don't have much time," said Julie. "Company is coming. Nasty company."

The speck of a bull-horned figure came hurrying across the sand toward the oasis.

"Saba just doesn't give up!" said Quill. "Knights, hurry!"

". . . bumpy . . . wumpy . . . woo-woo . . ."

"This is taking too long!" said Max suddenly. "I'm saving that seed!"

In a flash, he coiled one end of a length of spider silk around the tree trunk and clutched the other tightly.

"Max," whispered Keeah. "Max, wait —"

"Wish me luck!" he chirped. Then he leaped from the branches and yelled at the top of his lungs, "Ah-yeeee!"

In a flash, he swung down, grabbed the seed, released the rope, and landed in the sand.

The Snitchers squealed. "Attack! Attack!"

"Hey!" said Rolf. "Nobody attacks anybody without us! Forget the spell. Everyone, let's ah-yeeee!"

"Ah-*yeeee*!" they all yelled, leaping from the tree.

As soon as the Snitchers saw the giant knights, they screamed and wailed. Then the little puffy-panted creatures fell over one another trying to escape.

"Run away! Run away!" they cried. Before the knights could do a thing, the whole Snitcher band had scurried to their ponies and fled over the dunes in a cloud of dust.

The oasis battle was over in an instant.

Clutching the gizzleberry seed tightly, Max jumped to the squirming bag. When he opened it, Galen tumbled out, bound in chains from head to foot. He smiled when he saw Max.

"Somehow I knew you would save me!"

"*Inky . . . tinky . . . snoo!*" said Smee finally.

Plink! The chains fell to Galen's feet.

"Sir," said Rolf, "you need shorter spells!"

A cry echoed loudly in the distance, and everyone turned. Saba was charging toward the oasis.

At the same time, hooves thundered across the desert, and the enchanted blue pilkas leaped over a dune to the children.

"Max, take the seed," said Galen.

"Children, time is running out. Your caravan must continue. Go —"

As Saba ran faster and faster, lightning began to flash overhead. Soon, a storm of whirling sand and spinning wind swirled up around them.

"Hurry!" said Keeah. "To our next stop. Now!" The kids jumped on the pilkas and galloped straight into the storm.

As Galen and the knights formed a line between Saba and the kids, the phantom Saba slowed to a stop and shook his four fists violently. "I will — I will —"

But whatever Saba said was drowned out by the roaring winds. The children wrapped their robes around their faces to protect themselves from the blowing sand.

When the pilkas finally broke through the storm and raced onto the sand once more, the sun was low in the sky.

Evening was falling over the desert.

The travelers sped over dunes and into valleys for nearly an hour before stopping at a large wall of sand.

Keeah urged her pilka up the side, but it wouldn't go. None of the pilkas moved.

"Why aren't they going?" asked Eric.

Neal looked in every direction "This isn't right. There's nothing here but . . . nothing."

"Oh, dear," said Max. "What if the pilkas are lost? What if we aren't in the right place? The Talos, the ripple stick, and the gizzle-berry seed aren't enough to save the stairs —"

Suddenly, the ground thundered beneath their feet. A moment later, it happened again.

It felt as if something was moving toward them. Something heavy and huge.

Keeah sat bolt upright in her saddle.

Turning in every direction, she gasped. "I can't believe it. We *are* in the right place. Only the right place isn't here yet!"

Thoom . . . The sand shook again and again.

Suddenly, a giant tower wobbled up over the dune in front of them. Another tower followed the first, then another and another.

Then the massive gray foot of an enormous turtle slammed down over the top of a dune, shaking the ground like an earthquake.

"Tortu!" shouted Julie. "We've been seeing it all day! It's been wandering over Droon for centuries, until it reached this place, this time. Tortu is where we need to go!"

Thoom! Thooom! The turtle's big feet fell one after another.

"All aboard!" cried Max. He shot a sticky rope up at the turtle, and it clung fast to the massive shell.

As the great turtle's dome moved overhead, the kids leaped up from their pilkas and began to climb the silky rope. And the Magic City of Tortu, crawling for ages over Droon's vast deserts, pulled the children up and away.

Nine

The Domed City

"Wheeee!" cried Quill as they flew up toward the city.

With the help of Max's strong silk, it took the voyagers only minutes to climb Tortu's high walls. Once over the top, they dropped from roof to roof until they were safely huddled together in a narrow alley. The streets beyond them teemed with a strange assortment of creatures and people.

"Just like I remember it," whispered Neal, peering ahead into the crowd. "Galen called this place a den of magic and mystery."

Keeah smiled. "No wonder Galen's here. When we find him, we'll probably find the fourth treasure, too. Let's get going."

"Carefully," whispered Max.

Night was falling as they crept into the shadows. Strange spices scented the air, and the moist smell of gardens floated into the streets from hidden courtyards.

As they made their way through the streets, Eric remembered that Galen had also called Tortu a city of evil and danger. Three-legged hoolifans stomped around, growling like pirates. Magic traders barked out from their shadowy shops. Spell casters, snake charmers, jugglers, conjurors — some human, others not so human — all crowded the narrow passageways.

Mostly, there were the green-hooded guards who haunted every street, and who always seemed to be searching just for them.

"This is just as scary as the last time we were here," whispered Keeah.

"Scary?" said Quill. "I remember a song —"

"Sing later, hide now!" said Neal. "Here come the guards! Get into the shadows!"

They dashed into a side alley while a troop of very tall figures in green hoods stormed down the street, pushing every-one aside.

"Those guards work for Prince Maliban," whispered Keeah.

"Who later turns out to be Sparr him-self!" added Max with a quiver. "I remember that."

They all remembered their first time in the strange city.

The guards stomped by, inches from the children, staring out from under their hoods.

"The children are close by," growled one guard. "I sense them very near."

As soon as they passed, Eric saw someone dart down an alley on the far side of the street. He felt his fingers began to tingle.

"Holy cow!" he said. "Those guards aren't looking for us, they're looking for . . . *us*!"

Neal placed his palm on Eric's forehead. "Is your turban wound too tight or something?"

Eric smiled. "No, listen. We said that Tortu looks just like the last time we were here. I think that's because it *is* the last time we were here. Take a look —"

They all peered across the street and

saw five figures — themselves! — creep from one building to the next, climb to the roof of one low shop, and hop down to the next street.

"It *is* us!" whispered Julie. "I remember. We were searching for Hob the mask maker."

Eric watched himself slip away from his friends and disappear into a tangle of shops.

He remembered that, too. The first time he was in Tortu, he had just gained his powers. They were wild and uncontrollable. They made him feel different, and he wasn't sure he really wanted them. It was then that Galen had told Eric he was getting powers for a purpose.

"You know what this means," said Max, staring at his earlier self. "This means that the Galen we need to find —"

"Is right here," said a voice behind them. They turned, and there he was.

Galen was his old familiar self now, dressed in his full wizard's robe and cone hat. His bushy white beard hung nearly to his waist.

"Master!" said Max, hugging him tightly.

Galen hugged him back. "Max, friends, many years have passed since you all foiled the Snitchers. I know where the treasure you seek is. Then, more pressing business awaits me. Your other selves will need help in . . . twelve minutes. Hush —"

The hooded guards swept through the narrow streets again. Their eyes peered everywhere. The moment they passed, Galen glanced both ways. Then, holding a finger to his lips, he crept to the next corner. "Come —"

Everyone followed him in single file. Everyone except Eric. When he tried to follow his friends, he felt a hand holding him back. He turned, and the wizard was still there, looking at him.

Eric gasped. "What?" He looked at the corner, and Galen was there, too. "Wait . . . *what* —"

"Don't be afraid," said the wizard. "I sent a phantom with the others. I need to speak to you."

Eric's eyes bugged out. "A phantom? You know how to do that? That's a beast trick!"

The wizard shook his head. "It is not a trick, nor did it start with the beasts. It is — *was* — my mother's power. After Zara was kidnapped and failing in health, Ko stole it from her. But her sons, all of them, have this ability, if they only know how to use it."

"Sparr has it?" said Eric. "Does Urik have it, too?"

Galen nodded. "The whole line of wizards of which my mother Zara was queen."

"That's awesome —"

The wizard pulled Eric gently into a shadowed doorway. "I can tell your wizard powers have grown much since your first days here in this city."

"Maybe," he said. "But Droon needs a lot."

"Droon needs what you have, Eric," said Galen. "It needs all the help it can get. Since time is running out, I will speak plainly. When trouble is at its worst, close your eyes and see yourself do wonderful things. Then open your eyes, and do them. It's that simple. Do not lose faith. So much depends on you."

Eric felt a lump in his throat. He missed Galen very much. He wished the wizard was back with them all the time, like the old days.

"I had a scary vision this morning," Eric said quietly. "My town was nowhere. My house, my parents. Nothing was there. The staircase was gone. Everything was gone. And every vision I've ever had was of the future. Every vision I've ever had came true."

The wizard nodded slowly at Eric's words. "And yet here you are, trying to make sure that vision doesn't become real."

"But what if it's impossible to stop it?"

Galen peered into the teeming streets, then looked even more closely at Eric. "Impossible? No. All things are possible, Eric. All things. I do not know the future. I can only say —"

"They're nearby! Hurry!" The green guards raced toward the alley, calling to one another.

Galen turned, but Eric didn't move. "What? You can only say what?"

The wizard pulled him even deeper into the shadows. "I can only say that once, long ago, my vision of the future was also dark. I had lost a mother and two brothers. I was alone. And yet someone told me, 'What happens now is better than you can possibly imagine.' And those words proved more true than I could ever believe!"

"Galen . . ." said Eric. He paused.

He wasn't sure if he should tell the wizard that he was gone from their lives now. He wanted to say how he and his friends tried to search for him, but Ko kept making trouble for them.

Galen smiled. "Of course, I must have faith, too."

"Why?" asked Eric. "You can do anything."

"I must have faith so that if I disappear like the stairs, you will voyage as hard to find me!"

"We will!" said Eric, almost crying now.

Galen nodded. "Wait for the right time. And remember, all things are possible. You can do wonderful things."

With that, he moved away, invisibly joining his phantom at the corner, then racing down the street with the others.

Eric stood alone for a few seconds, close to tears. His fingers tingled and sparked as they hadn't done all day. Finally, he breathed deeply and began to smile.

"Eric!" whispered Keeah, her head appearing around the far corner. "Tick-tock!"

"Sorry," he said. "Coming!"

Galen led them down streets, past shops, around corners, slipping finally into a courtyard with a large fountain in the middle.

A noise came from the street outside.

"The fountain!" came the sudden shout of one of the green-hooded guards. Heavy footsteps echoed in the courtyard.

"They're coming," said Julie. "Stay in the shadows, everyone. Find the treasure. Oh, I can't believe I'm doing this —"

As the hooded guards stormed into the courtyard, Julie burst from the shadows and hopped onto the rim of the fountain. "Hey, guards. Looking for someone? Well, here I am. Come and get me!"

"Get her!" shouted all the guards at once.

Julie waited until they were close, then fluttered up to a nearby rooftop. Landing softly, she turned and waved. "Come on, guards, it's hide-and-seek. And you're It!"

She leaped off the roof, buzzed over the guards, then flew back out into the street. Shouting, the guards followed her, leaving the courtyard empty.

"She drew them all away!" said Max.

"Droon will remember this," said Galen, moving to the fountain. "And now, behold the treasure. . . ."

He bent over the fountain and pushed his hands into the water, but when he lifted them, they were not wet. Instead, the fountain was dry, and he held a small blue stone between his fingers. "The River Dragon," he said. "I have sought you for a long time."

"Is that the treasure?" asked Keeah.

Galen smiled. "The dragon has slept here in the fountain for centuries. Take it. When the time comes, you'll know what to do with it."

"Speaking of time," said Eric. "I think we're running out of it. The storm —"

The sun had set in the west, and flashes of blue light streaked across the evening sky.

Whoosh! — Julie flew breathlessly back to the courtyard. "We have to hurry. The pilkas are already racing toward the storm. And I spotted Saba moving through the streets."

Galen gave the tiny stone to Julie. "You helped us today, my dear. Take this from Tortu. Run. I'll create a diversion —"

At that moment, Saba stormed into the courtyard, beating his chest.

"He doesn't quit!" said Neal, backing up.

"Four treasures!" roared Saba. "I'll take them now!"

"You'll take this and like it!" said Galen. He leveled a powerful bolt of blue light at Saba, hurling him against the fountain.

"Fly!" said Julie. Grabbing her friends' hands, she pulled them up to the roof. They made their way across to the next roof, and the next.

Turning back, Eric saw Galen steady his aim to blast Saba again. But before the wizard could fire, the phantom faded away.

"Uh-oh," said Eric. "Saba's already going after the next treasure —"

"Hurry!" squeaked Quill. "I remember the next story and it's nearly time!"

"What was the next story?" asked Keeah.

"Midnight on the Silver Sand!" Quill said.

As the storm howled and the winds spun, the friends scrambled over the city wall and down to the turtle's great dome. The pilkas were racing alongside, and the little band leaped from Tortu onto their backs.

"Ride, ride, ride!" shouted Keeah.

Faster than the wind, the pilkas flew into the fifth whirling storm of light.

Ten

Midnight on the Silver Sand

When the lightning faded and the sand spun to earth, the pilkas touched down on the midnight desert of Eshku.

The air was cold. The sand stretched far in every direction. It was dull and gray in the moonless, starless night.

Mile after mile, the pilkas sped over the dunes. The caravan finally stopped.

Eric sensed something different this time.

"We're not alone," he whispered. "He's here. He's already here."

"I feel it, too," said Keeah. "Saba."

Creeping silently up the side of a great dune, the four kids, one spider troll, and one feather pen peered over the top and saw him.

Saba, the phantom, was standing atop a massive dune. He was motionless, staring up into the bleak sky, his three red eyes smoldering.

But Saba wasn't alone. Ko himself was nearby. Seated on a black throne, his three red eyes blazing in the darkness, he, too, was still and unmoving. Lying flat on the sand before him was an enormous black disk. It faced the sky like a giant dark eye, staring up from the depths of Droon itself like a bottomless pool.

Quill trembled. "I remember something. It's one of the oldest rhymes I can remember.

As the beast of beasts does sit,
His dark eye draws light into it."

No one said anything for a while.

"When are we?" asked Eric.

"I think we traveled *back* in time, not forward," said Quill. "I think we're at the beginning. This is Droon before Galen ever came."

Max shivered. "The air is very cold."

"If Saba had already found the fifth treasure, he wouldn't be here," said Keeah. "We got here in time."

Eric raised his hands. His fingers felt warm. He saw Keeah raise her hands, too. They were ready to strike if they had to.

But they didn't have to. Not yet.

If Ko or the phantom suspected the children were there, they didn't show it. Ko sat on his throne, and the phantom stood on his dune. Both were staring up at the blank sky.

"What are they looking at?" asked Neal. "They remind me of me, looking at a math problem on the board and not getting it. There aren't any stars. There's no moon —"

All at once, Eric remembered what Galen had said about the Talos. The *droomar* made it to watch the skies, the sun, the moon, everything.

He turned to Neal. "The Talos, quick!"

Frowning, Neal pulled out the twisted spectacles and handed them to his friend. Eric buffed them on his robe and put them on.

"What do you see?" asked Keeah.

Blinking into them, Eric saw something flash far away, high up in the great blank dome of the sky.

"Whoa . . ." he whispered.

It was nothing more than a pinpoint of light, a spark of violet in the vast darkness.

It flickered for a moment, then went out, and the sky was dark again. Minutes passed, then another flicker appeared. It, too, burned violet for a few seconds, then vanished.

Eric's heart raced. "It's Galen," he said.

Max turned to him. "What? How can you tell?"

"I don't know how I know, but I do," said Eric. "He's in the Upper World using the Wand of Urik, trying to create the stairs to Droon. But he can't find where the stairs should start. He needs . . . he needs our help."

"Our help?" said Keeah. "But how? He's all the way in another world. It's impossible —"

Eric's heart skipped a beat when Keeah said the word. *Impossible?*

Rrrrr . . . rrrrr . . . As Ko watched the tiny lights flickering in the heavens, the giant black disk began to rotate in the sand.

The phantom turned suddenly and saw the children. His horns spouted black flame, and he began to stride across the dunes toward them.

The disk turned faster. Saba came faster.

"Impossible?" Eric repeated. "No, it's not impossible. All things are possible. Galen told me that. All things!"

"Get ready," said Julie. "Saba's getting closer. Keeah, Eric, your fingers!"

But Eric was already remembering Galen's other words to him in the streets of Tortu.

See yourself do wonderful things.

He gave the Talos back to Neal and jumped to the crest of the dune. He saw the moon begin to rise above the horizon, its silvery light spreading over the sand.

The phantom was nearly upon them.

Keeah turned. "Eric, get ready to fight —"

He raised his hands. He would fight Saba. But he knew what else he had to do.

Mostly, he knew he *could* do it.

Jamming his eyes shut, Eric drew all his thoughts inside. He saw himself standing side by side with Keeah, aiming their hands together. He saw the phantom, heard him bellow — "You will not stop us!" — and charge full speed at them.

Even as he sensed Keeah, Julie, Neal, Quill, and Max standing firm on the dune next to him, he felt himself lifting up and out of his body.

He was no longer on the ground.

He felt as light as air. Lighter than air, as if birds drew him up over the moonlit desert.

As Eric floated above Droon toward the

sky, his other self and Keeah sent blast after blast at the bull-headed beast. He closed his eyes tight.

And he imagined wonderful things.

A moment later, he was running across the rocky ground of his world. Could he even explain how such a thing was possible? It didn't matter. All things were possible. Galen had told him that. And he knew it was true.

Closing his eyes for a second, he saw his other self battling the phantom, pushing him back across the sands of Eshku.

And yet, here he was, running toward the forest he had seen in his vision that morning.

Gethwing was wrong, he thought. *I am in two places at once!*

He staggered into an earthen hollow, smelled the wet ground, and felt cool air rush through his hair.

Breathless, he looked around. He remembered how devastated everything had seemed in his vision. But he knew something now that he hadn't known that morning. The world of his vision — and the world he was seeing now — were not what his town looked like after it had been destroyed, but *before* it had ever been built.

This was his world more than five centuries ago, at the moment Galen had first set foot here.

The downed trees had fallen, not from Gethwing's terrible rage, but in a storm. The rocks and boulders strewn across his neighborhood were the same ones that would be cleared away to build his house.

The moon was shining brightly now as he moved toward the nearby forest. Running to it, he could already hear the rainwater trickling from leaf to leaf, shedding droplets of water and making *pitting, patting* noises on the ground.

Best of all, there was no Gethwing here. There was only . . .

Crack! A branch snapped in the forest.

"I'm here," Eric said softly.

Although he felt he could listen in at any moment and hear the sounds of Saba roaring, Keeah yelling, Max shouting, and Neal yelping, the noise of Droon seemed far away.

"I'm here," he said again.

Then Eric watched a figure dart from tree to tree in the forest, a dark patch against the even darker background.

Fwit-fwit! The figure dashed out of the forest to a boulder, then to a nearer tree.

Closer. Closer.

Suddenly, the night air flashed again

with violet sparks. The light came from an object glowing in the figure's hand.

Eric smiled as he called out to his friend.

"Galen."

Eleven

Wonderful Things!

A moment later, a boy in a green tunic and green boots staggered up to Eric. His eyes were wide with wonder and gleaming in the violet light of the flowered wand in his hand.

"Eric?" he said breathlessly. "But . . . how did you get here?"

"I'm actually not here," said Eric. "I'm really down there." He pointed toward the earth. "Just call me the *phantom*!"

Galen smiled, surprised. "Phantom? Who taught you how to do that?"

"You did," said Eric. "You told me to close my eyes and see myself do wonderful things. Then open my eyes and do them. So I did."

Galen laughed. "That actually sounds smart. When did I tell you that?"

Eric tried to figure out just exactly *when* it was. But he gave up. "Later than now, I think. Anyway, it's a long story —" He laughed now, too. "A really long story, in fact!"

"I like stories," said Galen. "Especially long ones. Ones that never end."

Eric grinned. "Then you'll like this one!"

As simply as he could, Eric explained how more than five hundred years in the future Ko would curse the staircase, making it vanish. He told Galen of their voyage back through time to collect the five treasures.

"To make sure the stairs return," he said.

"The stairs that I haven't even made yet — they disappear?" asked Galen.

Eric nodded. "But then, none of what I just told you has actually happened yet."

"Sounds pretty strange," said Galen.

"A lot of it is strange," said Eric. "And scary. And dangerous. But most of what you'll find after you make the stairs to Droon is amazing and mysterious and incredible." Then, without thinking, he added, "What happens now is better than you can possibly imagine. . . ."

He trailed off, astonished to have said those words.

Galen smiled. "Better than I can possibly imagine. I like that. You know, I traveled five months across the sea, was shipwrecked three times, fought a sea serpent and an elephant king. But through it all, I knew I had to come right here."

Closing his eyes for a moment, Eric saw Julie flying over Saba, hurling fistfuls of sand in his face, but not slowing him down. And the real Ko was cranking his disk faster and faster.

"Galen, I have to go," he said finally. "I just wanted you to find the right place."

With that, he led Galen from the forest over broken trees, past boulders, and across a field, to a dip in the land between several rolling hills and a long gentle slope to the sea.

Turning, he walked several feet one way, again in another direction, then finally turned and walked back three steps.

Looking one final time in every direction, he nodded and smiled. "Here's the place. In about five hundred years, my house gets built right here. Julie and Neal and I find the staircase and meet you and Keeah and Max and —"

"What happens next is better than we can possibly imagine?" asked Galen.

Eric laughed. "Pretty much."

The wizard stepped to the spot. "So, I guess I'll be seeing you?"

"Oh, yeah. Lots."

Pointing the Wand of Urik at the ground, the boy wizard whispered words under his breath.

Shheeee! At the very moment the flower on the wand's tip lit up with purple light, and a single petal loosened and dropped to the earth, Eric felt that strange sensation coming over him again, as if he was being whisked away by a bird. Only this time, the bird was flying down through the ground and away.

When he popped open his eyes again, he was on the sand with his friends. He came into himself just as Saba sent another beam of flame and the top of the sand dune exploded in a splash of sand and fire.

Suddenly, Neal sprang to his feet. "Oh, my gosh. Look! There they are! The rainbow stairs!"

The next few seconds seemed to last forever.

A glow in the distant sky grew and grew until they could all see the magic staircase descending step by step toward Droon.

Step by step it came down directly toward Ko's spinning black disk.

Quill gasped. *"His dark eye draws light into it.* That's what it means!"

As they watched, streams of black fog rose from the disk like fingers, reaching for the stairs, drawing them to it.

"But no! He'll capture my master!" chittered Max. "Ko will control the staircase.

This can't happen! Everything we've worked for will be for nothing! What are we going to do?"

As the stairs descended toward Ko's whirling disk, Eric suddenly saw Neal wearing the Talos spectacles.

"The treasures . . ." he said. "According to Bodo, Galen said that without the treasures, the staircase wouldn't exist. What if the treasures are treasures because they helped make the staircase possible in the first place?"

"Are you saying we should use them?" asked Julie, pulling out the blue stone from her pocket.

The moment Saba saw the stone, he roared.

"That's it!" said Quill. "Throw it!"

With all her strength, Julie hurled the tiny stone. When it struck the sand, the stone burst into a river of bright, churning water. It roared like a dragon and swept around Saba, pulling him under for an instant. He came bobbing up and dragged himself to the River Dragon's far bank.

"We stopped him!" said Neal. "That's awesome!"

"The other treasures," said Eric.

Max pulled the seed from the pocket of his robe. "With a little water, I can grow a tree and show Galen where we are. I can send a signal!"

"Oh, this is good," said Quill, scribbling on his scroll. "Use the seed, use the seed!"

Quickly scooping a hole in the sand, Max planted the seed. In seconds, a gizzle-berry tree sprouted up from the ground and grew whole. Its berries — purple, rose, yellow, ruby, green, blue — gleamed like jewels in the dark night and sprayed light into the dark air.

"It's like a rainbow!" said Keeah. "I hope Galen can see it —"

All at once, Neal jumped. "Ahh! The Talos!" he cried. The spectacles jumped off his head, flipped and turned and wiggled and clicked in the air until both lenses stood end to end on their wire frame, facing each other. The Talos shot into the air and hovered over the blazing tree, shining the berries' light with a powerful force. A sharp rainbow-colored beam of light shot up into the night sky, reaching nearly up to the stairs.

"Whoa!" gasped Neal. "The Talos is like a supersonic spotlight."

"The ripple stick!" said Quill, scribbling furiously. "Theesha's musical stick must do something, too!"

Keeah took the little stick covered with metal rings from her belt. The moment she shook the stick — *shing-a-ling!* — the splashing, tinkling sound of the tiny rings rippled into the light shooting up from the Talos and formed the shape of steps.

The shape of steps!

"Unbelievable!" Eric gasped.

The stairs of rainbow light kept rolling upward farther and farther as Galen's stairs kept coming down. Then, as if drawn by their own mirror image, Galen's stairs curved away from Ko's revolving disk.

"The staircase is turning," said Julie. "Of course it is! From the very first time we found it, it curved through the air to Droon."

The two sets of stairs met in midair, high above the earth. When the steps joined, they formed a single staircase much brighter than each half had been separately. At that moment, the moon edged up over the horizon, and turned the desert sand to silver.

Now, young Galen came racing down from the very top of the gleaming staircase. At first he descended two steps at a time, then in longer, faster strides.

Meanwhile, Saba was still trying to cross the water, but the River Dragon churned more violently, tossing him roughly back to its far shore.

"No!" Ko roared. He leaped up from his throne. With his thunderous voice, he bellowed at the children. "You shall not win! You shall not —"

He leaped across the sand to Saba's side. Together, the eyes of the Emperor and his phantom burned like a furnace.

"Blast the beasts, Eric!" shouted Keeah. "Blast them as you never have before —"

Eric joined Keeah at the top of a dune overlooking the charging emperor and his phantom. His hands were raised and sprinkling silver sparks.

Finally, he let go with all the power in him.

KA — WHAMMM!

The sound of the explosion rocked the desert. Ko was knocked back a hundred feet, landing facedown on his black disk. Saba was hurled across the ground until he was completely covered in silver sand.

The emperor of the beasts and his phantom howled on the ground but were not able to get up.

Neal, Julie, and Max dashed to their friends. Quill leaped up from Eric's turban.

"We did it!" cried Neal.

"So did he," said Keeah, turning.

They all looked back just in time to see Galen jump from the bottom of the stairs into Droon for the very first time. Looking back up at the stairs, he smiled and waved the wand. The staircase twinkled, sparked, and faded into the silver night.

A moment later, Galen leaped easily over the river, raced across the shimmering sand, and was gone.

Quill wiggled. "A happy ending. And a new beginning. I like that!"

Ko climbed to his feet, and Saba melted into him. When the emperor saw that both the stairs and Galen were gone, he sank to the ground again. Bowing his horned head, he began pounding his four fists on the sand. *Thump-thump . . . thump-thump . . .*

"Maybe we should leave now," said Neal.

Julie rushed to the river, put her hands into it, and pulled. The river vanished and was a stone again.

"One last thing." Eric ran to where the staircase had been. Lying on the sand was a small purple object. Trembling, he picked it up. It was the petal from the Wand of

Urik he had seen fall the moment Galen had created the staircase.

"The fifth treasure," he said. "We need this to make the staircase come again."

"Speaking of coming again," said Quill. "I think we all know what's coming now!"

KKKK! Light flashed across the night sky. The magical storm was upon them again.

Keeah gave a sharp whistle. "To the pilkas, everyone!" she shouted. "Let's ride!"

The enchanted pilkas charged toward them, and together the five friends leaped into their saddles and raced into the storm.

No sooner had they flown into the whirling wind than they flew out again, right into the Kalahar Valley. It was nearly midnight. The city of Ro was tilting out of the clouds and diving toward the children. From the sight of King Zello and Queen Relna waving from the Tower's top, the kids knew they were back in the present again.

"Hurry!" cried Vasa, waving next to them, "our time is up —"

As the enchanted pilkas flew up from the ground and into the city, the clouds tore open again. And the black palace of Emperor Ko dived at them, too, its fires blazing.

Twelve

Beyond the Clouds

The flying city of Ro zigzagged away from the emperor's speeding palace, its engines sputtering and smoking.

Whoosh! The enchanted pilkas soared straight to the top of the Tower and circled while the kids hopped down one by one. Along with King Zello, Queen Relna, Khan, and the Guardians, were row upon row of the Zorfendorf royal guard.

"You're safe!" cried Relna, hugging Keeah.

"With all five treasures," said Max.

"Archers!" boomed Zello.

With one swift motion, the soldiers aimed their arrows, and Relna ran along the wall, zapping the tip of each one with a spark of sapphire light. The points blazed in the midnight air.

"Wizard fire!" gasped Quill. "Ko won't like that."

Keeah nudged Eric. "Shall we give Ko a little wizard fire of our own?"

Eric smiled. "Oh, yeah!"

Just as Ko's terrifying black ship bore down on them, the two wizards joined with Relna.

"Wait . . ." said Zello, holding his hand up. "Wait . . . wait . . ."

All at once, the flying city turned and faced Ko's palace.

"And . . . now!" shouted the king.

WHOOOOM! Fifty sizzling arrows — and the combined blasts of Relna, Keeah, and Eric — lit up the midnight sky.

At once, Ko's palace plummeted toward the earth. A wailing stream of beasts shot out the ship's back door just before it slammed into the ground and burst into a thousand flaming pieces.

"Bull's-eye!" yelled Eric.

A cheer went up from the Tower of Memory. Ko's terrible floating palace had been completely destroyed.

As the flying city of Ro hovered above the wreckage, Ko staggered to his feet on the ground below. He roared a command to his beasts.

Massing together, they collected what was left of his ship and dragged it back across the ground to the Dark Lands.

"I can't believe it," said Keeah. "We did it!"

"He'll be back," said Zello. "But not tonight. For the moment, this battle is over."

"While another battle begins in the Upper World," said Relna. "Let's hurry."

The next ten minutes — before the hour of midnight struck — were a blur of activity. The beautiful flying city of Ro landed safely in the Kalahar Valley, and the Rovians cheerfully began the work of collecting diamonds.

As they did, Bodo and Vasa called the children and Max to the front steps of the palace, where the voyagers returned their caravan clothes.

"You have protected Droon's history today," said Bodo. "Each of you, in his or her own way, has played a part. All of Droon is thankful."

"There are so many stories and legends in Droon's past," said Vasa. "And you have been characters in quite a few of them."

"Don't I know it!" said Quill. "I'd have a cramp from writing them all down, except that I don't have hands!"

Neal grinned suddenly. "If we've been in legends, does that mean that we're *legendary*?"

Bodo laughed. "It does! But we've known this for a long, long time!"

"All right!" Neal cheered.

With a signal from the little Rovian with the yellow helmet, Vasa nodded. "So the time has come. Our diamonds are on board; the Tower of Memory is safe. Droon's history is repaired. The treasures must be restored."

Bodo opened the empty chest.

Max placed the gizzleberry seed in the very bottom, and Keeah laid Theesha's ripple stick next to it. Neal handed over the Talos, which had transformed itself back into a pair of spectacles, while Julie put the small stone by its side.

When Eric held out the petal from the Wand of Urik, Vasa shook his head. "Not yet. This petal is the greatest treasure of them all. It serves another purpose as well. The time has come to bring the staircase back."

As the moon rose right overhead, the friends gathered in a small circle in the courtyard of the Guardians' palace.

"This is it," said Eric, glancing at Neal and Julie and Keeah. "I hope this works. . . ."

"I hope so, too," said Julie.

"Hey, you gotta have faith," said Neal.

Together, the five friends held the petal. It jiggled and wiggled.

It flew out of their hands, dropped to the ground, and — *whoosh!* — the rainbow staircase curved up before them, rising to the sky more blindingly bright than ever before.

"Yes! It's back!" cried Eric.

"And it's as beautiful as it was the night Galen created it," said Julie.

Keeah smiled. "We should know. We were there."

"Helping Galen through five hundred years has made this one moment possible," said Max. "It's so . . . magical!"

Neal shook his head slowly. "Five hundred years. Man, we are *old*!"

Eric's heart was racing. "Are we ready?"

Khan jumped. "Me, for sure!"

"And me!" added Max.

The queen smiled. "We're all going!"

Looking at his friends, Eric laughed. "Why do I feel another adventure coming?"

Keeah laughed, too. "Because there's always another adventure!"

The moon glowed brightly as the small army of Droon's heroes said good-bye to Quill, the Guardians, and the citizens of Ro and raced up the stairs to find Sparr and Gethwing and bring them back to Droon.

Before they were halfway up, the city of Ro began to rise quickly under the silver moon. Its thousands of lights twinkled and flashed and finally dissolved into the night sky.

Leaping up the stairs again, Eric remembered — just like Galen had — the very first time he had entered Droon. He had been so full of excitement and wonder at his new adventure.

Now, as they all raced up the stairs together — up beyond the clouds of

midnight and through the morning stars —
he felt the same about his home.

It was full of adventure now, too.

"To the Upper World!" Eric called out.

"To the Upper World!" everyone
cheered.

About the Author

Tony Abbott is the author of more than sixty books for young readers, including the *Danger Guys* and *The Weird Zone* series, and the middle-grade novel *Kringle* (Scholastic Press, 2005). Since childhood he has been drawn to stories that challenge the imagination, and, like Eric, Julie, and Neal, he often dreamed of finding doors that open to other worlds. Now that he is older — though not quite as old as Galen Longbeard — he believes he may have found some of those doors. They are called books. Tony Abbott was born in Ohio and now lives with his wife and two daughters in Connecticut.

For more information about Tony Abbott, the continuing saga of Droon, and his other books, visit *www.tonyabbott-books.com*.

Want to get in on a really big secret?

nter to win a signed

Secrets of Droon

oster!

en lucky winners
ill receive a
ecrets of Droon post-
r signed by the au-
nor—plus
complete
ollection of
ecrets of Droon
ooks!

Name_____ Age_____

Address_____

City_____ State/Zip_____

e this form to fill out your name,
dress, and age, and send to:

Secrets of Droon Sweepstakes
c/o Scholastic Inc
P.O. Box #715
New York, NY 10013

www.scholastic.com

■ SCHOLASTIC

From the beloved author of The Secrets of Droon comes the epic story of the young Kris Kringle!

In a time when goblins and elves still roamed the earth, a lost orphan boy discovers his destiny: to fight the forces of darkness—and change the world forever.